U0010695

泰戈爾 著

杜力璇 譯

流螢集
FireFlies

好讀出版

他的博大的溫柔的靈魂我敢說永遠是人類記憶裏的一次靈績。

他是不可侵凌的，不可逾越的，他是自然界的一個神秘的現象。

他是一派浩瀚的大水，來從不可追尋的淵源，在大地的懷抱中終古的流著，不息的流著，我們只是兩岸的居民，憑藉這慈恩的天賦，灌漑我們的田稻，蘇解我們的消渴，洗淨我們的污垢。

——摘錄自徐志摩於一九二四年五月十二日在北京的演講

（當時，在中國訪問的泰戈爾即將離華）

《流螢集》的詩句，

源自造訪中國與日本時，

人們要我在扇子或絲布上寫下的一些字句。

——拉賓德拉納．泰戈爾

寫於一九二六年十一月七日

匈牙利，巴拉頓福瑞

I

我的幻想如團團螢火，
一點一點亮晶晶，
在黑暗中幽微閃爍。

My fancies are fireflies,—

Specks of living light

twinkling in the dark.

2

路旁三色菫聲聲喚，
盼不來世人匆匆一瞥，
只能黯然低吟碎不成章的詩。

The voice of wayside pansies,

that do not attract the careless glance,

murmurs in these desultory lines.

5

歡樂自沉睡大地掙脫束縛，
匆匆沒入數不盡的葉片，
終日歡快飛舞。

Joy freed from the bond of earth's slumber

rushes into numberless leaves,

and dances in the air for a day.

3

沉睡的心之穴，
夢境正在織就，
築以白晝大漠商旅遺落的斷片。

In the drowsy dark caves of the mind
dreams build their nest with fragments
dropped from day's caravan.

4

春天吹得花瓣紛飛四落，
誰教花兒不念來日之結果，
只思須臾花枝招展。

Spring scatters the petals of flowers
that are not for the fruits of the future,
but for the moment's whim.

6

我重如泰山的作品終將淹沒，
我的話語輕如鴻毛，
或可在時間洪流中輕舞飛揚。

My words that are slight
may lightly dance upon time's waves
when my works heavy with import have gone down.

7

無人知曉的心之蛾，生出了薄翼，

在落日餘暉中，以道別之姿飛翔。

Mind's underground moths grow filmy wings

and take a farewell flight in the sunset sky.

8

蝴蝶看重的不是數以月計，

而是每個頃刻須臾，

是以牠擁有的時間足夠了。

The butterfly counts not months but moments,

and has time enough.

II

我的愛如陽光照拂著你，

為你帶來蓬勃生輝的自由。

Let my love, like sunlight, surround you

and yet give you illumined freedom.

9

我的思考如電光石火，
攜著福至心靈的笑，
乘坐教人驚詫的羽翼而來。

My thoughts, like sparks, ride on winged surprises,

carrying a single laughter.

10

樹木深情凝視自己美麗的影子，
卻注定捕捉無望。

The tree gazes in love at its own beautiful shadow

which yet it never can grasp.

12

白晝是彩色泡泡，
浮盪在黑沉沉的夜幕之上。

Days are coloured bubbles

that float upon the surface of fathomless night.

13

我怯然地奉上捐獻，
不敢要祢記得，
興許祢由此記住了它們也未可知。

My offerings are too timid to claim your remembrance,
and therefore you may remember them.

14

假若我的名將是個負擔，
請從禮物上抹去它吧，
但勿忘歌頌我。

Leave out my name from the gift if it be a burden,
but keep my song.

17

莊嚴肅穆的神殿，
跑出了孩子，坐在塵土裡，
神明入神地瞧著他們嬉戲，
竟忘了祭司的存在。

From the solemn gloom of the temple
children run out to sit in the dust,
God watches them play
and forget the priest.

15

四月像個孩子，
拿花在塵土上寫下圖畫般的象形文字，
並隨手拂拭以忘卻。

April, like a child,
writes hieroglyphs on dust with flowers,
wipes them away and forgets.

16

回憶是個女祭司，
她殺死現在，
將它的心獻祭給已逝往昔的神殿。

Memory, the priestess,
kill the present
and offers it heart to the shrine of the dead past.

18

順著思緒之流，我心靈光乍現，
正如川流不息的溪澗
倏然激起一組清脆的音符。

My mind starts up at some flash
on the flow of its thoughts,
like a brook at a sudden liquid note of its own
that is never repeated.

19

在山裡，靜謐奔騰著，
以探究自己有多高；
在湖中，湧動靜止著，
以思索自己有多深。

In the mountain, stillness surges up
to explore its own height;
in the lake, movement stands still
to contemplate its own depth.

20

黑夜臨走前的一吻，
落在晨曦緊閉的睡眼上，
曉星兀自含羞地發光發熱起來。

The departing night's one kiss
on the closed eyes of morning
glows in the star of dawn.

21

女孩，
你美得像顆將熟的果實，
那緊致來自你渾身彆扭的奧祕。

Maiden, thy beauty is like a fruit
which is yet to mature,
tense with an unyielding secret.

黎明

無止盡地匯聚到來

同一輪太陽每一次新生

都像踏上嶄新大地

22

不知為何而悲的憂傷，

恍若置身暗啞的黑暗時光，

不聞悅耳鳥鳴，只得蟋蟀蟲聲唧唧。

Sorrow that has lost its memory
is like the dumb dark hours
that have no bird songs
but only the cricket's chirp.

24

臂彎雖擁大地新娘入懷，

天空深渺依舊，既高且闊。

Though he holds in his arms the earth-bride,
the sky is ever immensely away.

25

上帝以愛尋覓夥伴，

撒旦要的是服從祂的奴隸。

God seeks comrades and claims love,
the Devil seeks slaves and claims obedience.

23

偏執試圖將真實拽在手心，
不想卻捏死了它。
盡心盡力想鼓舞一盞畏縮的燈，
偉闊夜幕點亮了所有星子來幫忙。

Bigotry tries to keep truth safe in its hand
with a grip that kill it.
Wishing to hearten a timid lamp
great night lights all her stars.

26

將樹木牢牢盤根在自己身邊，
是土地所要的回報。
天空則毫無所求，一任自由。

The soil in return for her service
keeps the tree tied to her,
the sky asks nothing and leaves it free.

27

寶石永流傳，
不因恆久遠而自豪，
而在兀自閃耀的璀璨一瞬。

Jewel-like the immortal
does not boast of its length of years
but of the scintillating point of its moment.

28

孩子活在恆常如新的神祕歲月裡，

不因歷史的喧囂擾嚷而蒙塵。

The child ever dwells in the mystery of ageless time,

unobscured by the dust of history.

29

萬物的每一步都帶著微笑，

輕快地穿越時光而去。

A light laughter in the steps of creation

carries it swiftly across time.

32

當內心的安寧捋起袖子蕩掃穢物，

風暴便起。

When peace is active sweeping its dirt,

it is storm.

30

疏離的他，在早晨走向我，

夜晚將他帶走時，我們已然離得更近。

One who was distant came near to me in the morning,

and still nearer when taken away by night.

31

白色夾竹桃與粉紅夾竹桃相遇，

開心地以自家方言聊了開來。

White and pink oleanders meet

and make merry in different dialects.

33

湖泊低伏，倚著小山，

噙滿愛的淚水苦苦哀求，

哭倒在不動如山的腳邊。

The lake lies low by the hill,

a tearful entreaty of love

at the foot of the inflexible.

34

神賜的孩子笑著在

隨性的雲朵和倏忽的光影間遊戲。

There smiles the Divine Child

among his playthings of unmeaning clouds

and ephemeral lights and shadows.

35

輕風低聲問蓮花：「你藏有什麼祕密？」

睡蓮說：「我就是我，

一旦被奪走，就不復存在。」

The breeze whispers to the lotus,

"What is thy secret?"

"It is myself," says the lotus,

"Steal it and I disappear."

38

暴君主張他有扼殺自由的自由，

他倒是把自由留給了自己。

The tyrant claims freedom to kill freedom

and yet to keep it for himself.

36

風暴挾著自由與
渾身受縛的樹幹，
攜手在飄搖枝條間舞了一場。

The freedom of the storm and the bondage of the stem
join hands in the dance of swaying branches.

37

茉莉的花朵，
象徵她對太陽含羞吐露的愛意。

The jasmine's lisping of love to the sun
is her flowers.

39

厭倦了身處的天堂，
神羨慕起人來。

Gods, tired of their paradise, envy man.

17

40

煙靄造山揉成了雲，
石頭砌雲壘成了山，
——此乃浮世一瞬的幻想。

Clouds are hills in vapour,
hills are clouds in stone,—
a phantasy in time's dream.

41

神等著自己的宮殿用愛修築，
世人卻帶來了石頭。

While God waits for His temple to be built of love,
men bring stones.

44

揮別昨夜的淚，今日的心微笑了，
就像沐浴在雨後陽光下
濕得發亮的樹。

My heart to-day smiles at its past night of tears
like a wet tree glistening in the sun
after the rain is over.

42

我以頌歌觸摸神明，
正如高山以瀑布觸碰遙遠的大海。

I touch God in my song
as the hill touches the far-away sea
with its waterfall.

43

未經一番與雲霧的角力，
光線哪能成就五彩繽紛。

Light finds her treasure of colours
through the antagonism of clouds.

45

我感謝豐碩了我生命的樹木，
卻忘了向常保我內心柔嫩的小草道謝。

I have thanked the trees
that have made my life fruitful,
but have failed to remember the grass
that has ever kept it green.

46

有一沒有二著實空虛，

有二相伴才踏實。

The one without second is emptiness,

the other one makes it true.

47

生命犯下的過錯哭喊著要得到寬恕，

只為能被導回正軌，成就完整的自我。

Life's errors cry for the merciful beauty

that can modulate their isolation

into a harmony with the whole.

50

池塘自幽深處獻上

寫在睡蓮上的頌詩，

太陽說，它們美極了。

The pond sends up its lyrics from its dark in lilies,

and the sun says, they are good.

48

被迫遠離家園居然得感激，

說是換來了多麼華美堅固的牢籠。

They expect thanks for the banished nest

because their cage is shapely and secure.

49

無論你是什麼樣的人，

我都將償還愛裡無邊的情債。

In love I pay my endless debt to thee

for what thou art.

51

你對豪傑義士的不敬詆毀，

乃自取其辱；

你對尋常百姓的卑劣中傷，

則使人蒙害。

Your calumny against the great is impious,

it hurts yourself;

against the small it is mean,

for it hurts the victim.

52

大地綻放了第一朵花，

那是發給未來之歌的邀請。

The first flower that blossomed on this earth

was an invitation to the unborn song.

53

花一般雲蒸霞蔚的黎明褪去，

成分純粹扎實的光之果太陽登場。

Dawn—the many-coloured flower—fades,

and then simple light-fruit,

the sun appears.

54

體能陷入自我懷疑，

扼殺了內在發出的哭喊。

The muscle that has a doubt of its wisdom

throttles the voice that would cry.

心的安寧
總在黑暗與光明之間
浮沉

55

勁風試圖強攻火焰，
反倒吹熄了它。

The wind tries to take the flame by storm
only to blow it out.

56

人生這齣戲不斷流轉，
人生的玩具不斷被拋下，
終致遺忘。

Life's play is swift,
Life's playthings fall behind one by one
and are forgotten.

59

黑夜是位蒙著面紗的新娘，
恬靜等待四處浪蕩的光明
回到她心上。

Darkness is the veiled bride
silently waiting for the errant light
to return to her bosom.

57

我的鮮花呀，

顢頇之人筆挺西裝上的鈕孔

不是你該安歇插放的天堂。

My flower, seek not thy paradise

in a fool's buttonhole.

58

我的新月啊，

你雖姍姍來遲，

我的夜鳥仍清醒恭候。

Thou hast risen late, my crescent moon,

but my night bird is still awake to greet thee.

60

為了上達天聽，

大地不斷努力讓樹長得更高更高。

Trees are the earth's endless effort to

speak to the listening heaven.

25

61

自我解嘲之際，
身上重擔輕了。

The burden of self is lightened
when I laugh at myself.

62

弱者也會變得可怕，
因為他們懷著滿腔的怒意
想展現剛強。

The weak can be terrible
because they try furiously to appear strong.

65

蔚藍天空渴慕著翠綠大地，
天地間的風嘆道：「唉！」

The blue of the sky longs for the earth's green,
the wind between them sighs, "Alas."

63

天堂颳大風，

船錨拚命扒緊泥巴，

我的小船挺起胸膛緊偎錨鍊。

The wind of heaven blows,

The anchor desperately clutches the mud,

and my boat is beating its breast against the chain.

64

死路只有一條，

活著卻有千千萬萬種樣子。

神死去，信仰萬流歸宗。

The spirit of death is one,

the spirit of life is many.

When God is dead religion becomes one.

66

在炫然日光下，白晝遏抑自己的痛苦，

留待繁星高掛的夜裡燃燒自己。

Day's pain muffled by its own glare,

burns among stars in the night.

67

夜晚如處子，群星簇擁

默然敬畏

那聖潔不可侵的孤寂。

The stars crowd round the virgin night

in silent awe at her loneliness

that can never be touched.

68

瑞影金雲傾其所有，歡送太陽離去，

只餘一抹微弱殘笑，迎候升起的月。

The cloud gives all its gold

to the departing sun

and greets the rising moon

with only a pale smile.

71

昔日暴政橫行，

如今孩子在其廢墟上打造娃娃屋。

With the ruins of terror's triumph

children build their doll's house.

69

行善之人來到神殿門口，
心懷著愛的人進到了殿堂。

He who does good comes to the temple gate,
he who loves reaches the shrine.

70

花朵啊，
憐憫這隻並非蜜蜂的小蟲吧，
牠的愛是份錯愛與負擔。

Flower, have pity for the worm,
it is not a bee,
its love is a blunder and burden.

72

撐過漫漫白晝的冷眼相待，
燈盞只盼夜晚給予熱焰親吻。

The lamp waits through the long day of neglect
for the flame's kiss in the night.

29

73

羽毛心滿意足地懶躺於塵埃之中，
忘卻了自己的天空。

Feathers in the dust lying lazily content
have forgotten their sky.

74

獨一無二的花啊，
毋須妒羨四周多不勝數的荊棘。

The flower which is single
need not envy the thorns
that are numerous.

75

偽善魔人擎著道德大旗，
既深且重地傷了這個世界。

The world suffers most from the disinterested tyranny
of its well-wisher.

為了萬物生生不息
白晝獻上金琴
交由沉默的群星彈奏

76

我們為生存付出所有，

終贏來了自由。

We gain freedom when we have paid the full price

for our right to live.

77

秋夜裡劃過的一道流星，

是你偶然的心意，

炸裂了我波心的小宇宙。

Your careless gifts of a moment,

like the meteors of an autumn night,

catch fire the depth of my being.

80

世界是顆不斷變幻的泡沫，

浮盪在靜寂之海無聲的表面。

The world is the ever-changing foam

that floats on the surface of a sea of silence.

78

信念的種籽在心底發芽，

應許著不日終將證明的生命奇蹟。

The faith waiting in the heart of a seed

promises a miracle of life

which it cannot prove at once.

79

春天猶在冬日門前徘徊，

芒果花卻不合時宜地魯莽衝撞，

注定了她的早夭。

Spring hesitates at winter's door,

but the mango blossom rashly runs out to him

before her time and meets her doom.

81

分離的兩岸

在深邃的淚海之歌中，

彼此唱和。

The two separated shores mingle their voices

in a song of unfathomed tears.

82

江河奔流入海，
在深沉的棲止中
找到了完滿。

As a river in the sea,
work finds its fulfilment
in the depth of leisure.

83

我一直在落櫻繽紛的路上徘徊，
但我的愛，你寬恕了我，
還捎來綻放容顏的杜鵑花。

I lingered on my way till thy cherry tree lost its blossom,
but the azalea brings to me, my love, thy forgiveness.

86

萬物誕生於夜之謎團，
投身更為縹渺的日之祕境。

Birth is from the mystery of night
into the greater mystery of day.

84

嬌羞的小小石榴花蕾，

今日滿臉緋紅地躲藏面紗下，

明日待我離去，

便即蛻變成一朵熱情的花。

Thy shy little pomegranate bud,

blushing to-day behind her veil,

will burst into a passionate flower

to-morrow when I am away.

85

權力的笨拙，使壞了鎖匙，

連十字鎬也出動。

The clumsiness of power spoils the key,

and uses the pickaxe.

87

我的這些紙船

願舞於時光漣漪之上，

不知所終。

These paper boats of mine are meant to dance

on the ripples of hours,

and not to reach any destination.

35

88

漂泊之歌逸出我心，
在你愛的歌聲裡尋覓歸巢。

Migratory songs wing from my heart
and seek their nests in your voice of love.

89

布滿危疑的矛盾之海，
環繞著人類安居的小小確切之島，
挑戰地問世人敢不敢航向未知。

The sea of danger, doubt and denial
around man's little island of certainty
challenges him to dare the unknown.

92

黎明

無止盡地匯聚到來，
同一輪太陽每一次新生，
都像踏上嶄新大地。

The same sun is newly born in new lands
in a ring of endless dawns.

90

愛
以寬容做為懲罰，
以懾人的沉默斷喪了美。

Love punishes when it forgives,
and injured beauty by its awful silence.

91

高處不勝寒，
你如高山，世人仰止。

You live alone and unrecompensed
because they are afraid of your great worth.

93

神明的世界，有生有死，生生不息，
泰坦巨人的干戈世界，因祂們本身而崩毀。

God's world is ever renewed by death,
a Titan's ever crushed by its own existence.

94

發著光的螢火蟲忙於探索塵土，

從不知頭頂滿天星斗。

The glow-worm while exploring the dust

never knows that stars are in the sky.

95

今日之樹，

古老的花，

花兒身上含藏著遠古洪荒種籽的訊息。

The tree is of to-day, the flower is old,

it brings with is the message

of the immemorial seed.

98

昨日之愛摒棄了棲所，

我今日的愛找不到歸處。

My love of to-day finds no home

in the nest deserted by yesterday's love.

96

每朵綻放的玫瑰，

全是不朽春日裡

那朵玫瑰捎來的問候。

Each rose that comes brings me greetings

From the Rose of an eternal spring.

97

當我工作時，神彰顯我，

當我歌唱時，祂傾慕於我。

God honours me when I work,

He loves me when I sing.

99

痛苦的火

跨過自己的哀傷，

為我的靈魂

探照出一條明亮道路。

The fire of pain traces for my soul

A luminous path across her sorrow.

100

小草生生不息，
比山崗更綿長。

The grass survives the hill
Through its resurrections from countless deaths.

101

你就這樣消失在我生命裡，
藍天裡觸不到的撫摸
晃動暗影中看不見的風之身影，
全都是你。

Thou hast vanished from my reach,
leaving an impalpable touch in the blue of the sky,
an invisible image in the wind moving
among the shadows.

102

榮榮枯枝
春天心懷憐憫給了它一吻，
孤葉在枝椏上震顫不已。

In pity for the desolate branch
spring leaves to it a kiss that fluttered in a lonely leaf.

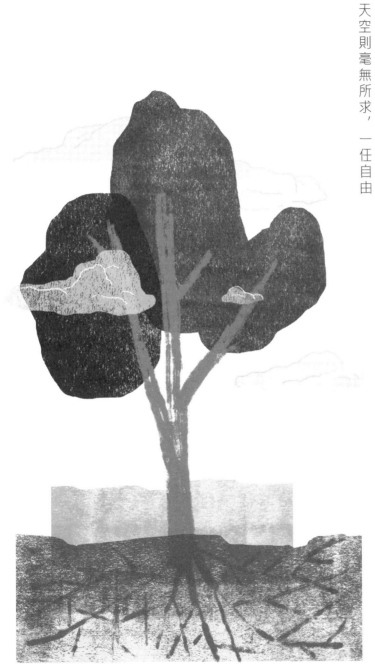

將樹木牢牢盤根在自己身邊
是土地所要的回報
天空則毫無所求，一任自由

103

花園裡，陰影默默愛著太陽，

花兒猜中了祕密含笑不語，

樹葉群聚竊竊私語。

The sky shadow in the garden

loves the sun in silence,

Flowers guess the secret, and smile,

while the leaves whisper.

104

天空中，羽翼痕跡未曾稍留

我很快樂

曾有過這麼一場飛翔。

107

玫瑰才剛對太陽說：

「我會永遠記住你。」

花瓣便片片落入塵土。

While the rose said to the sun,

"I shall ever remember thee,"

her petals fell to the dust.

I leave no trace of wings in the air,
but I am glad I have had my flight.

105

螢火蟲在枝葉間閃耀，
天上群星訝異極了。

The fireflies, twinkling among leaves,
make the stars wonder.

106

山看似為霧靄所敗，
實則巍然不動。

The mountain remains unmoved
at its seeming defeat by the mist.

108

對於高遠不可及者，
山，十足演繹了
大地的絕望之姿。

Hills are the earth's gesture of despair
for the unreachable.

109

你花間的棘刺刺痛了我，

噢，美人，

我仍心存感激。

O Beauty,

I am grateful.

Though the thorn in thy flower pricked me,

110

宇宙很清楚，

少數不比多數少。

The world knows that the few

are more than the many.

113

美

在完美的鏡子前顧影姿容，

映照出了真理的微笑。

Beauty is truth's smile

when she beholds her own face

in a perfect mirror.

111

我的朋友，

我的愛不該讓你感到負擔，

愛一旦付出便是完滿。

Let not my love be a burden on you, my friend,

know that it pays itself.

112

黎明在黑暗門前撥弄琴弦，

當太陽現身，

她即瀟灑離去。

Dawn plays her lute before the gate of darkness,

and is content to vanish when the sun comes out.

114

露珠對太陽的認識，

不出自己小而圓的身體。

The dew-drop knows the sun

only within its own tiny orb.

45

115

絕望情思自永世廢棄的蜂房逸出，

如蜂群飛舞，嗡嗡縈繞我心，

尋求著我的共鳴。

Forlorn thoughts from the forsaken hives of all ages,

swarming in the air, hum round my heart

and seek my voice.

116

沙漠築起高牆，

將自己囚在無邊的荒涼裡。

The desert is imprisoned in the wall

of its unbounded barrenness.

119

林間燃起了火焰，

花朵中火星四濺，

這是大地獻上的祭火。

The earth's sacrificial fire

flames up in her tress,

scattering sparks in flowers.

117

在細葉的震顫中，
我感到氣流隱隱地舞著，
從葉間躍動的金光裡，
我察覺天空祕密的心跳。

In the thrill of little leaves
I see the air's invisible dance,
and in their glimmering
the secret heart-beats of the sky.

118

當我讚賞你美好的天賦，
你竟驚喜得像棵滿開的樹。

You are like a flowering tree,
amazed when I praise you for your gifts.

120

森林，這朵大地之雲，
直著身軀向天際送上自己的靜默，
天上的雲下凡來，
化身陣陣驟雨共唱和。

Forests, the clouds of earth,
hold up to the sky their silence,
and clouds from above come down
in resonant showers.

47

121

這個世界透過圖像對我說話，

我的靈魂以樂音回應了祂。

The world speaks to me in pictures,

my soul answers in music.

122

夜空忙著

將無以計數的星星串成念珠，

訴說對太陽的思念。

The sky tells its beads all night

on the countless stars

in memory of the sun.

125

畫筆為迎合窄幅的畫布，

不惜呈現窄縮後的真實。

The obsequious brush curtails truth

in deference to the canvas which is narrow.

123

夜晚的黑，如喑啞般痛苦，

黎明的黑，一派沉靜安寧。

The darkness of night, like pain, is dumb,

the darkness of dawn, like peace, is silent.

124

驕傲將緊蹙的眉頭鐫刻在石頭裡，

愛情則在花朵中獻出臣服。

Pride engraves his frowns in stones,

love offers her surrender in flowers.

126

山丘渴慕遙遠的天際，

盼望能如雲朵一直緊隨在側。

The hill in its longing for the far-away sky

wishes to be like the cloud

with its endless urge of seeking.

127

為了替灑翻的墨水開脫，

他們把白天拼寫成黑夜。

To justify their own spilling of ink

they spell the day as night.

128

當好人身上有利可圖，

利潤這才對美德咧齒露笑。

Profit smiles on goodness

when the good is profitable.

131

我的雲朵在黑暗中憂傷，

忘了是自己將太陽遮蔽。

My clouds, sorrowing in the dark,

forget that they themselves

have hided the sun.

129

自我意識過剩的泡沫，

質疑起大海的真理，

狂妄大笑到撐破了自己，

終究化作虛無。

In its swelling pride

the bubble doubts the truth of the sea,

and laughs and bursts into emptiness.

130

愛情是個無盡的謎團，

萬物無以名之。

Love is an endless mystery,

for it has nothing else to explain it.

132

當神明來到跟前，

要求獻上天賦長才，

人類這才發現自己有多豐富

。

Man discovers his own wealth

when God comes to ask gifts of him.

51

133

你留下的回憶像火焰，
照亮我這盞
與你仳離的孤燈。

You leave your memory as a flame
to my lonely lamp of separation.

134

我來為你獻上一朵花，
你卻要我整座花園，
——都拿去吧。

I came to offer thee a flower,
but thou must have all my garden, —
It is thine.

137

愛說出來
仍然是祕密，
只有在愛裡的人能解密。

Love remains a secret even when spoken,
for only a lover truly knows that he is loved.

135

這幅帶有光之記憶的圖畫，

是陰影珍藏的寶貝。

The picture – a memory of light

treasured by the shadow.

136

太陽零死角

暴露在自己普照的光芒裡，

是以要對他扮鬼臉容易得很。

It is easy to make faces at the sun,

He is exposed by his own light in all directions.

138

歷史慢慢地扼殺真相，

卻又在飽經痛苦折磨的懺悔中

匆匆地想讓它復活。

History slowly smothers its truth,

but hastily struggles to revive it

in the terrible penance of pain.

真理熱愛自己的極限

在那裡，它遇見了美

139

每日薪餉是我工作的回報，

我等待著

以愛攢得人生的終極價值。

My work is rewarded in daily wages,
I wait for my final value in love.

140

美懂得說：「夠了。」

粗俗吵嚷著要更多。

Beauty knows to say, "Enough,"
barbarism clamours for still more.

143

當玫瑰盛放，愛情是美酒，

當玫瑰花瓣凋敝、巨大飢餓來臨，

愛情搖身成了麵包。

In the bounteous time of roses love is wine, —
it is food in the famished hour
when their petals are shed.

141

神不要我做祂的僕人，

而要我同祂一般服務眾人。

God loves to see in me, not his servant,

but himself who serves all.

142

夜的黑

與白晝融洽得很，

卻與霧之晨不甚合拍。

The darkness of night is in harmony with day,

the morning of mist is discordant.

144

在異鄉，

一朵不知名的花對詩人說：

「我的愛，

「難道我們不是踏在同一片土地上嗎？」

An unknown flower in a strange land

speaks to the poet:

"Are we not of the same soil, my lover?"

145

我能夠愛我的神，
是因為祂給了我
否定祂的自由。

I am able to love my God
because He gives me freedom to deny Him.

146

為懇求陽春白雪，
我那走調的琴弦
不住懊惱痛苦地呼喊著。

My untuned strings beg for music
in their anguished cry of shame.

149

我的樹蔭供過客乘涼，
我的果實在等待那個人來。

The shade of my tree is for passers-by,
its fruit for the one for whom I wait.

147

人類何以不啃食書本，

蠹蟲深感不解，深以為愚。

The worm thinks it strange and foolish

that man does not eat his books.

148

今日烏雲密布，

不朽的天際垂得很低，

鬱鬱沉思的額頭

印上了一抹聖潔的悲傷暗影。

The clouded sky today bears the vision

of the shadow of a divine sadness

on the forehead of brooding eternity.

150

夕陽霞彩滿天，

紅撲撲的大地像顆熟透的果實，

等著被夜晚摘採。

Flushed with the glow of sunset

earth seems like a ripe fruit

ready to be harvested by night.

151

為了宇宙萬物，
光明同意與黑暗共結連理。

Light accepts darkness for his spouse
for the sake of creation.

152

蘆笛等待著主人吹奏，
主人卻自尋蘆笛去了。

The reed waits for his master's breath,
the Master goes seeking for his reed.

155

貪求結果，
錯失花開的美。

The greed for fruit misses the flower.

153

對瞎盲的筆而言，

握著自己書寫的那隻手並不真實，

它的書寫也毫無意義。

To the blind pen the hand that writes is unreal,

its writing unmeaning.

154

不毛的胸膛

長不出鮮花獻給月亮，

大海為此懊惱捶胸。

The sea smites his own barren breast

because he has no flowers to offer to the moon.

156

神明在祂的繁星廟裡，

等候世人帶來智慧的明燈。

God in His temple of stars

waits for man to bring him his lamp.

61

157

管束在樹裡的火，長成了花朵。

那逃離枷鎖的火，火焰漸殘，

死滅在荒寂的灰爐裡。

The fire restrained in the tree fashions flowers.

Released from bonds, the shameless flame

dies in barren ashes.

158

天空未曾設下牢籠捉捕月亮，

倒是她身上的自由縛住了她。

The sky sets no snare to capture the moon,

it is her own freedom which binds her.

159

天色大亮，

青草尖上露珠晶瑩剔透，

天光沒打算放過這處小圓蒼穹。

The light that fills the sky

seeks its limit in a dew-drop on the grass.

噢·蒼穹
我在窗前虔敬地與祢同在
毋須踏入曠野
因那是專屬於祢的國度

160

家財萬貫是生命中不能承受之重，

濟弱扶傾才真正圓滿生命。

Wealth is the burden of bigness,

Welfare the fulness of being.

161

剃刀裡的小刀片

自認鋒利無邊，

連太陽它也不放在眼裡。

The razor-blade is proud of its keenness

when is sneers at the sun.

164

雲端的彩虹或許壯觀，

但灌木叢間飛舞的小小蝴蝶

身影毋寧更動人。

The rainbow among the clouds may be great

but the little butterfly among the bushes is greater.

蝴蝶有空向睡蓮追愛，
蜜蜂哪來閒工夫，得勤工貯蜜才行。

The butterfly has leisure to love the lotus,
not the bee busily storing honey.

孩子，是你將風和水的潺潺細語、
花兒無言的祕密、雲朵的夢想，
以及對奇蹟般清朗黎明的默然凝望，
都帶進了我的心。

Child, thou bringest to my heart
the babble of the wind and the water,
the flowers' speechless secrets, the clouds' dreams,
the mute gaze of wonder of the morning sky.

霧靄別有用心地在清晨身旁織網，
想捕捉他，使他昏頭轉向。

The mist weaves her net round the morning,
captivates him, and makes him blind.

166

曉星輕聲問黎明：

「告訴我，你的到來全是為了我。」

「是為了你，」她說，

「還有為那些不知名的花朵。」

The Morning Star whispers to Dawn,

"Tell me that you are only for me."

"Yes," she answers,

"And also only for that nameless flower."

167

天空始終浩渺無垠，

好讓大地攜著夢想打造自己的天堂。

The sky remains infinitely vacant

for earth there to build its heaven with dreams.

170

美

在含苞待放的蓓蕾，

在未熟的甜蜜花蕊，

微笑著。

Beauty smiles in the confinement of the bud,

in the heart of a sweet incompleteness.

168

一旦聽說

自己只是個等待成就圓滿的碎片，

新月或許會疑心地淺笑吧。

Perhaps the crescent moon smiles in doubt

at being told that it is a fragment

awaiting perfection.

169

黃昏原諒白晝犯的錯，

為自己贏得了安寧。

Let the evening forgive the mistakes of the day

and thus win peace for herself.

171

你那輕率的愛情羽翅

拂掠過我的向日葵，

從未問它願否獻出花蜜。

Your flitting love lightly brushed with its wings

my sun-flower

and never asked if it was ready to surrender its honey.

67

172

葉子如此靜默，

環繞花朵而生，

每朵花都是它心愛的言語。

Leaves are silences

around flowers which are their words.

173

樹木支起了千年歲月，

恍若偉岸一瞬。

The tree bears its thousand years

as one large majestic moment.

176

當死去之人的德行事蹟變成了豐功偉業，

死神大笑，

祂虛榮寶庫裡的收藏又添了一筆。

Death laughs when the merit of the dead is exaggerated

for it swells his store with more than he can claim.

174

道路盡頭的大廟並非我奉祭的對象，

我要獻給路旁拐角處

每每使我驚嘆的那些小神龕。

My offerings are not for the temple
at the end of the road,

but for the wayside shrines
that surprise me at every bend.

175

我的愛，

你的笑容像一朵奇花臉上綻開的笑，

單純卻又難解。

Your smile, my love, like the smile of a strange flower,
is simple and inexplicable.

177

海岸為追不到輕風嘆息，

這會風兒正催著船隻渡海呢！

The sigh of the shore follows in vain
the breeze that hastens the ship across the sea.

69

178

真理熱愛自己的極限，

在那裡，它遇見了美。

Truth loves its limits,

for there it meets the beautiful.

179

在分隔你我的兩岸之間

橫亙著一片喧囂之海，

那是我一直渴望橫渡的

波濤洶湧的本我。

Between the shores of Me and Thee

there is the loud ocean, my own surging self,

which I long to cross.

182

為了萬物生生不息，

白晝獻上金琴，

交由沉默的群星彈奏。

Day offers to the silence of stars

his golden lute to be tuned

for the endless life.

180

占有權
愚蠢地吹噓自己
擁有享樂的權利。

The right to possess boasts foolishly
of its right to enjoy.

181

玫瑰渾然不覺自己有多重要，
竟羞慚地為身上長刺道歉。

The rose is a great deal more
than a blushing apology for the thorn.

183

聰明人懂得如何去教，
糊塗之人只知道要揍。

The wise know how to teach,
the fool how to smite.

184

圓圈之舞一圈又一圈

永無休止,

圓心卻靜寂不動。

The centre is still and silent in the heart

of an eternal dance of circles.

185

法官身上散發光芒,

和其他人燈裡的油相較,

竟還自認是公平的化身。

The judge thinks that he is just when he compares

the oil of another's lamp

with the light of his own.

188

聽,是森林的聲音,

它隱身花中,祈求著自由。

Listen to the prayer of the forest

for its freedom in flowers.

186

草地上的花嫉妒她，
那朵被囚禁在國王王冠上的花
只得苦笑。

The captive flower in the King's wreath
smiles bitterly when the meadow-flower envies her.

187

積雪的重負有山承擔，
融雪成流由世人共享。

Its store of snow is the hill's own burden,
its outpouring of streams is borne by all the world.

189

親暱生狎侮，
你得越過這道阻隔，
用愛來理解我。

Let your love see me
even through the barrier of nearness.

190

天地萬物興致高昂地忙這忙那，

是為了能更起勁地玩樂。

The spirit of work in creation is there

to carry and help the spirit of play.

191

樂器得隨身攜帶，不時數算耗費的成本，

從不明白那可是為了音樂啊，

這樣的人生跟聾了沒兩樣，

是場悲劇。

To carry the burden of the instrument,

count the cost of its material,

and never to know that it is for music,

is the tragedy of deaf life.

192

信念是鳥兒，

在黎明前的黑暗中感受到光亮，

唱起了啁啾之歌。

Faith is the bird that feels the light

and sings when the dawn is still dark.

世界是一幅幅美麗的畫
我用心靈的樂音
與之唱和

193

黑夜，

我為祢帶來白晝的空杯觥，

望祢用寒涼的黑暗滌淨，

以迎接嶄新的黎明慶宴。

I bring to thee, night, my day's empty cup,

to be cleansed with thy cool darkness

for a new morning's festival.

194

山上的冷杉沙沙作響，

昇華它與風暴相互角力的記憶，

淬鍊成一首歌詠和平的讚美詩。

The mountain fir, in its rustling,

modulates the memory of its fights with the storm

into a hymn of peace.

197

記憶從言語面前遁逃，

在生命的晦暗深處

砌起一座座孤獨的巢穴。

In the shady depth of life

are the lonely nests of memories

that shrink from words.

195

當我造反，
神明加入戰局彰顯我，
當我萎靡，
祂則毫不理睬我。

God honoured me with his fight
when I was rebellious,
He ignored me when I was languid.

196

識見偏狹之人還以為，
已把智慧汪洋都舀進了他那一汪小塘。

The sectarian thinks
that he has the sea
ladled into his private pond.

198

我的愛
在忙碌的白晝找到力量，
在和諧的夜晚享受安寧。

Let my love find its strength
in the service of day,
its peace in the union of night.

77

199

生命的力量隱身草葉，

為不知名的光

送上無聲的讚美詩。

Life sends up in blades of grass

its silent hymr of praise

to the unnamed Light.

200

夜晚的滿天星斗，

是我對一朵朵白晝蔫花的憑弔。

The stars of night are to me

the memorials of my day's faded flowers.

203

海岸低聲對大海說：

「把你的海浪掙扎著要說的話，

「都寫下來給我吧！」

大海用泡沫寫了一遍又一遍，

卻又在暴怒的絕望中

將這些詩句一手揩去。

The shore whispers to the sea:

"Write to me what thy waves struggle to say."

The sea writes in foam again and again

and wipes off the lines in a boisterous despair.

201

打開你的門，讓該走的走吧，

攔著不放手，

終將讓這份磨耗變得粗鄙。

Open thy door to that which must go,

for the loss becomes unseemly when obstructed.

202

真正的目標

並非達致極限，

而要徹底地探求無限。

True end is not in the reaching of the limit,

but in a completion which is limitless.

204

我生命的琴弦因你的觸摸而顫抖，

人生的樂章自此有你有我。

let the touch of thy finger thrill my life's strings

and make the music thine and mine.

79

205

我的內在世界宛如一顆包覆著的果實，

在悲喜交織中成熟，掉落太古洪荒的土壤，

融入天地萬物的自然更迭。

The inner world rounded in my life like a fruit,

matured in joy and sorrow,

will drop into the darkness of the original soil

for some further course of creation.

206

萬物的推展有其作法，

力量的施展蘊有節奏，

人的存在含藏著意義。

Form is in Matter, rhythm in Force,

meaning in the Person.

209

上天啊，

願我對真理的信賴、

對完美的憧憬，

有益袮打造萬物。

My faith in truth, my vision of the perfect,

help thee, Master, in thy creation.

207

有人尋求智慧，有人追求財富，

我尋覓的是友情，

好讓我一路歌頌。

I seek thy company so that I may sing.

There are seekers of wisdom and seekers of wealth,

208

如同葉落，

我將言語流瀉大地，

開出無聲的思想之花，

常伴你的靜默。

As the tree its leaves, I shed my words on the earth,

let my thoughts unuttered flower in thy silence.

210

曲終人散之際，

我在完美和諧的愛裡，

為你獻上

生命花果帶給我的滿滿歡愉。

All the delights that I have felt

in life's fruits and flowers

let me offer to thee at the end of the feast,

in a perfect union of love.

211

有些人很優秀，

搜索枯腸探求祢真理的意義；

而我很快樂，

能細細聆聽祢演奏的樂音。

Some have thought deeply and explored

the meaning of thy truth,

and they are great;

I have listened to catch the music of thy play,

and I am glad.

212

樹木是有羽翼的精靈，

鬆開種籽的束縛，橫越未知，

追尋自己生命的歷險。

The tree is a winged spirit

released from the bondage of seed,

pursuing its adventure of life

across the unknown.

213

蓮花向天空獻上美麗，

青草一心一意侍奉大地。

The lotus offers its beauty to the heaven,

the grass its service to the earth.

葉子如此靜默
環繞花朵而生
每朵花都是它心愛的言語

214

青澀果實

在太陽催熟的親吻下變得疏懶，

貪婪地緊握枝椏不放。

the miserliness of the green fruit clinging to its stem.

The sun's kiss mellows into abandonment

215

火焰和我內心素燒的土燈

相遇了，

真是教人讚嘆的光明啊！

The flame met the earthen lamp in me,

and what a great marvel of light!

218

不想在黑暗中徒勞搜索，

我心依舊懷抱信念，

相信天色將明，

真理亦將清晰自明。

Let me not grope in vain in the dark

but keep my mind still in the faith

that the day will break

and truth will appear

in its simplicity.

216

謬論跟真理住得很近，

導致我們常弄混。

Mistakes live in the neighbourhood of truth

and therefore delude us.

217

雲朵嘲笑彩虹，

說它只是個華而不實的新寵。

彩虹平靜以對：「我跟太陽一樣貨真價實。」

The cloud laughed at the rainbow

saying that is was an upstart

gaudy in its emptiness.

The rainbow calmly answered,

"I am as inevitably real as the sun himself."

219

度過漫漫寂靜夜，

我聽見浪跡的黎明輕叩我心，

它帶著希望回來了。

Through the silent night

I hear the returning vagrant hopes of the morning

knock at my heart.

220

我的新戀情翩然降臨，

帶著從昔日愛情

精釀的永恆飽滿而來

My new love comes

bringing to me the eternal wealth of the old.

221

大地仰望著月亮，讚嘆道，

天地萬物的悅耳天籟，

竟都讓她收進了笑容裡。

The earth gazes at the moon and wonders

that she should have all her music in her smile.

224

人類一邊拿神明的花朵織花環，

一邊說那些花都是自己的。

Man claims God's flowers as his own

when he weaves them in a garland.

222

白晝出於好奇，瞪大了眼睛看，

把星星都嚇跑了。

Day with its glare of curiosity

puts the stars to flight.

223

噢，蒼穹，

我在窗前便能虔敬地與祢同在，

毋須踏入曠野，

那是專屬於祢的國度。

My mind has its true union with thee, O sky,

at the window which is mine own,

and not in the open

where thou hast thy sole kingdom.

225

湮沒的城市

光禿俯臥在改朝換代的太陽底下，

為自己失卻了所有頌歌，

羞愧難當。

The buried city, laid bare to the sun of a new age,

is ashamed that it has lost all its songs.

226

彷彿太陽罩上黑袍遮光，藏身地底，

我的心一直痛著，

痛得失去了存在的意義。

我傷痛的心

在愛情突如其來的觸動下，

彷若受春天召喚，換下面紗，

穿得花枝招展，

投入這場生氣勃勃的狂歡。

Like my heart's pain that has long missed its meaning,

the sun's rays robed in dark

hide themselves under the ground.

228

從土壤的束縛中釋放而出，

那並非

樹木要的自由。

Emancipation from the bondage of the soil

is no freedom for the tree.

Like my heart's pain at love's sudden touch,
they change their veil at the spring's call
and come out in the carnival of colours,
in flowers and leaves.

227

我的生命是支空洞長笛，
等待著最後的吹奏，
有如置身群星出現前
那片亙古的黑暗。

My life's empty flute
waits for its final music
like the primal darkness
before the stars came out.

229

人生故事的錦繡，
以人間生活的各種羈絆織就，
絲線斷斷續續，牽絆分分合合。

The tapestry of life's story is woven
with the threads of life's ties
ever joining and breaking.

230

話語沒法捕捉的那些情思，

都棲止在我的詩歌和舞蹈裡。

Those thoughts of mine that are never captured by words

perch upon my songs and dance.

231

今夜，我的靈魂迷失在

一棵內心沉靜的樹裡，

那樹

兀自挺立在無邊的瑟瑟低語裡。

My soul tonight loses itself

in the silent heart of a tree

standing alone among the whispers of immensity.

234

我的生命像帶有音孔的蘆笛，

穿透充盈著希望與收穫的孔隙，

奏出繽紛的旋律。

My life like the reed with its stops,

has its play of colours

through the gaps in its hopes and gains.

232

大海將貝殼
沖上死亡的荒涼沙灘，
——創意的生命遭到了華麗的浪費。

Pearl shells cast up by the sea
on death's barren beach,—
a magnificent wastefulness of creative life.

233

太陽的光芒為我打開世界的大門，
愛的光輝開啟了裡頭的寶藏。

The sunlight opens for me the world's gate,
love's light its treasure.

235

都說默默致上最高敬意，
我對你的心意，
不該被區區謹申謝忱搶了去。

Let not my thanks to thee
rob my silence of its fuller homage.

91

236

孩子
是人生各種盼望
的喬裝化身。

Life's aspirations come
in the guise of children.

237

枯萎的花朵嘆道，
春天已然消逝永不回。

The faded flower sighs
that the spring has vanished for ever.

238

在我的生命花園裡，
財富宛如光影，
從不曾被採集，更無從貯藏起。

In my life's garden
my wealth has been of the shadows and lights
that are never gathered and stored.

我的新戀情翩然降臨
帶著從昔日愛情
精釀的永恆飽滿而來

239

你收下了我的果實，
那就是我最珍貴的收穫。

The fruit that I have gained for ever
is that which thou hast accepted.

240

茉莉花知道，
太陽是她在天堂的手足。

The jasmine knows the sun to be her brother
in the heaven.

243

我失去了一隻以網捕捉的蝴蝶，
而正在花間輕快飛舞的這隻
將永遠屬於我。

The butterfly flitting from flower to flower
ever remains mine,
I lose the one that is netted by me.

241

光雖然來自很久以前，卻很年輕；

影雖活在當下，卻一出生就老了。

Light is young, the ancient light;

shadows are of the moment, they are born old.

242

我感覺到，

當白晝將盡，

生命詩歌的渡筏將帶我到彼岸，

在那裡，我當明白一切。

I feel that the ferry of my songs at the day's end

will bring me across to the other shore

from where I shall see.

244

自由的鳥兒啊，

你的歌聲傳入我沉睡的巢，

教我疲憊的翅膀

做了個直上雲彩的飛翔之夢。

Your voice, free bird, reaches my sleeping nest,

and my drowsy wings dream of a voyage to the light

above the clouds.

95

245

在人生這齣戲，
我不明白自己扮演的角色，
畢竟其他人的角色，
我也一點頭緒都沒有。

I miss the meaning of my own part
in the play of life
because I know not of the parts
that others play.

246

花瓣落盡，
花朵得到了果實。

The flower sheds all its petals
and finds the fruit.

249

為了尋覓妥帖的表達，
心靈不斷在作聲與沉默之間拿捏，
正如蒼穹也一直在黑暗與光明間轉換。

The mind ever seeks its words
from its sounds and silence
as the sky from its darkness and light.

247

離去前，
我將頌歌留給

每年春天回歸綻放的金銀花，

以及年年從南方歡快吹來的夏日薰風。

I leave my songs behind me
to the bloom of the ever-returning honeysuckles
and the joy of the wind from the south.

248

枯葉在土壤中迷失了自己，
其實早已融入森林的生命裡。

Dead leaves when they lose themselves in soil
take part in the life of the forest.

250

看不見的黑暗正吹奏長笛，
將光明的旋律送進無窮的
星星與太陽，
思想與夢想。

The unseen dark plays on his flute
and the rhythm of light
eddies into stars and suns,
into thoughts and dreams.

251

我要歌頌你，
因為我愛上了你的歌唱。

My songs are to sing
that I have loved Thy singing.

252

沉默之聲觸碰我的言語，
我懂得了他，
也識得了自己。

When the voice of the Silent touches my words
I know him and therefore I know myself.

255

當死神前來對我低語：「你的時候到了。」
我會對祂說：

「我一直活在愛裡，而不只是時間裡。」

當祂問：「你的詩歌還會流傳下去嗎？」
我將如此回答：「我想不會。

「但我知道只要吟唱，
「就能找到片刻的永恆。」

When death comes and whisper to me,
"Thy days are ended,"
let me say to him, "I have lived in love
and not in mere time."

253

我要向那些

知道我不完美卻仍然愛我的人，

送上最後致意。

My last salutations are to them

who knew me imperfect and loved me.

254

愛的禮物沒法給予，

它得等待接納。

Love's gift cannot be given,

it waits to be accepted.

256

「我來點燃我的燈，」

星星說，

「而毋須盤算對驅走黑暗有沒有幫助。」

"Let me light my lamp,"

says the star,

"and never debate

if it will help to remove the darkness."

He will ask, "Will thy songs remain?"

I shall say, "I know not, but this I know

that often when I sang, I found my eternity."

2 5 7

走到旅程的盡頭之前，
願我終覓得一以貫之之道，
而任這身皮囊隨眾生飄颺，
於變動不居的潮水中浮沉流逝。

Before the end of my journey
May I reach within myself
the one which is the all,
leaving the outer shell
to float away with the drifting multitude
upon the current of chance and change.

沒有人
看得見我的羽翼
唯有我清楚自己
每一次的人間飛翔

國家圖書館出版品預行編目資料

流螢集／泰戈爾（Rabindranath Tagore）著；杜力璇譯
——初版——臺中市：好讀，2017.10
面；公分，——（典藏經典；108）
譯自：Fireflies
ISBN 978-986-178-410-6（平裝）

867.51   105022453

好讀出版

典藏經典 108

流螢集
Fireflies

作　　者／泰戈爾 Rabindranath Tagore
譯　　者／杜力璇
內頁繪圖／尤淑瑜
扉頁圖畫／徐悲鴻
總 編 輯／鄧茵茵
文字編輯／簡伊婕
內頁編排／王廷芬
行銷企畫／劉恩綺
發 行 所／好讀出版有限公司
臺中市 407 西屯區何厝里 19 鄰大有街 13 號
TEL:04-23157795 FAX:04-23144188
http://howdo.morningstar.com.tw
（如對本書編輯或內容有意見，請來電或上網告訴我們）
法律顧問／陳思成律師

戶名：知己圖書股份有限公司
劃撥帳號：15060393
服務專線：04-23595819 轉 230
傳眞專線：04-23597123
E-mail：service@morningstar.com.tw
如需詳細出版書目、訂書，歡迎洽詢
晨星網路書店 http://www.morningstar.com.tw

印　　刷／上好印刷股份有限公司 TEL:04-23150280
初　　版／西元 2017 年 10 月 1 日
定　　價／200 元
如有破損或裝訂錯誤，請寄回臺中市 407 工業區 30 路 1 號更換（好讀倉儲部收）

Published by How Do Publishing Co., Ltd.
2017 Printed in Taiwan
All rights reserved.
ISBN 978-986-178-410-6

讀者回函

只要寄回本回函，就能不定時收到晨星出版集團最新電子報及相關優惠活動訊息，並有機會參加抽獎，獲得贈書。因此有電子信箱的讀者，千萬別吝於寫上你的信箱地址

書名：流螢集

姓名：＿＿＿＿＿＿ 性別：□男□女 生日：＿＿年＿＿月＿＿日

教育程度：＿＿＿＿＿＿＿＿＿＿

職業：□學生 □教師 □一般職員 □企業主管
　　　□家庭主婦 □自由業 □醫護 □軍警 □其他＿＿＿＿＿＿＿

電子郵件信箱（e-mail）：＿＿＿＿＿＿＿＿ 電話：＿＿＿＿＿

聯絡地址：□□□＿＿＿＿＿＿＿＿＿＿＿＿

你怎麼發現這本書的？

□書店 □網路書店（哪一個？）＿＿＿＿＿＿□朋友推薦 □學校選書

□報章雜誌報導 □其他＿＿＿＿＿＿＿＿＿＿

買這本書的原因是：＿＿＿＿＿＿＿＿＿＿＿

□內容題材深得我心 □價格便宜 □封面與內頁設計很優 □其他＿＿＿＿

你對這本書還有其他意見嗎？請通通告訴我們：

＿＿＿＿＿＿＿＿＿＿＿＿＿＿＿＿＿＿

你買過幾本好讀的書？（不包括現在這一本）

□沒買過 □1～5本 □6～10本 □11～20本 □太多了

你希望能如何得到更多好讀的出版訊息？

□常寄電子報 □網站常常更新 □常在報章雜誌上看到好讀新書消息

□我有更棒的想法＿＿＿＿＿＿＿＿＿＿

最後請推薦五個閱讀同好的姓名與 E-mail，讓他們也能收到好讀的近期書訊：

1.＿＿＿＿＿＿＿＿＿＿＿＿＿＿＿＿

2.＿＿＿＿＿＿＿＿＿＿＿＿＿＿＿＿

3.＿＿＿＿＿＿＿＿＿＿＿＿＿＿＿＿

4.＿＿＿＿＿＿＿＿＿＿＿＿＿＿＿＿

5.＿＿＿＿＿＿＿＿＿＿＿＿＿＿＿＿

我們確實接收到你對好讀的心意了，再次感謝你抽空填寫這份回函

請有空時上網或來信與我們交換意見，好讀出版有限公司編輯部同仁感謝你！

好讀的部落格：http://howdo.morningstar.com.tw/

好讀的臉書粉絲團：http://www.facebook.com/howdobooks

好讀出版有限公司　編輯部收

407 台中市西屯區何厝里大有街 13 號
電話：04-23157795-6　傳眞：04-23144188

────── 沿虛線對折 ──────

購買好讀出版書籍的方法：

一、先請你上晨星網路書店http://www.morningstar.com.tw檢索書目
　　或直接在網上購買

二、以郵政劃撥購書：帳號15060393　戶名：知己圖書股份有限公司
　　並在通信欄中註明你想買的書名與數量

三、大量訂購者可直接以客服專線洽詢，有專人爲您服務：
　　客服專線：04-23595819轉230　傳眞：04-23597123

四、客服信箱：service@morningstar.com.tw